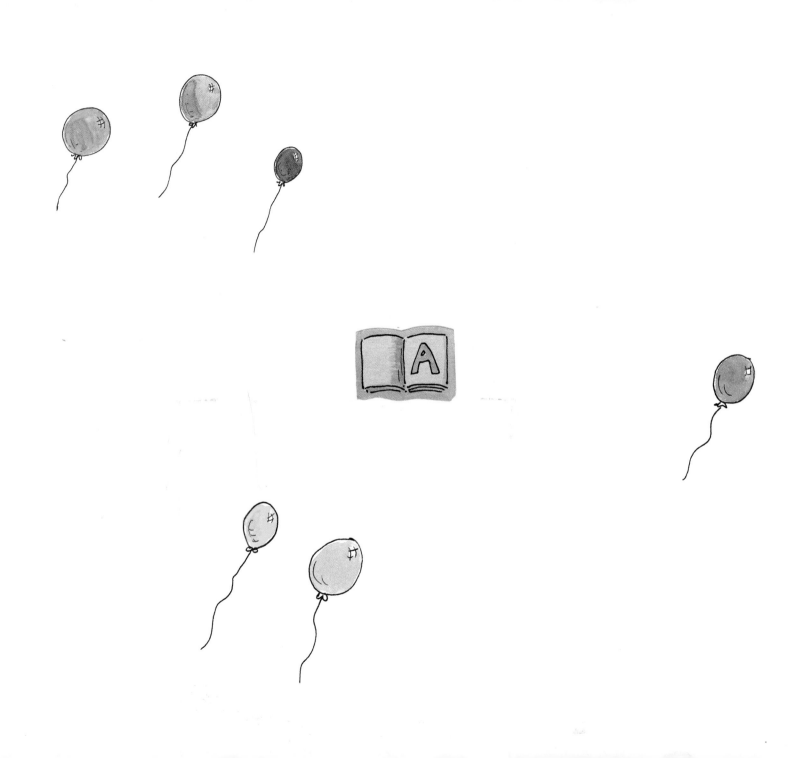

A

Amiable Amy, Alice, and Andie
Ate all the anchovy sandwiches handy.

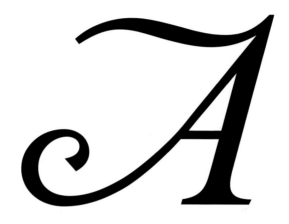

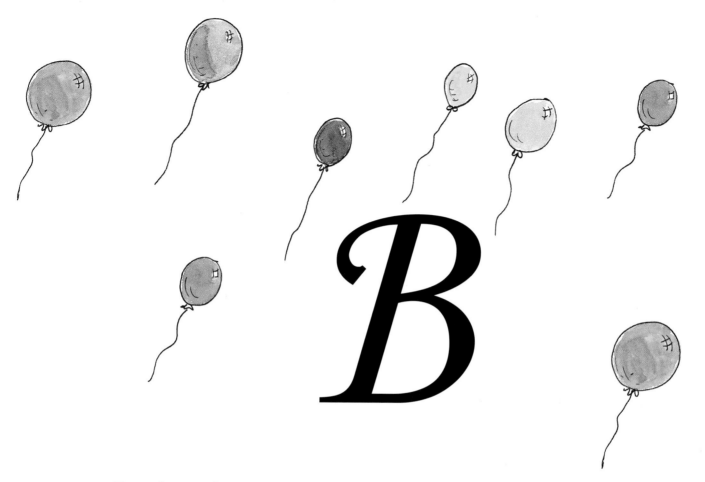

Bad Baby Bubbleducks beat up his bed
With bashed-up bananas and old moldy bread.

C

Clunky Clarissa, all clingy and clueless,

Left California and now she is shoeless.

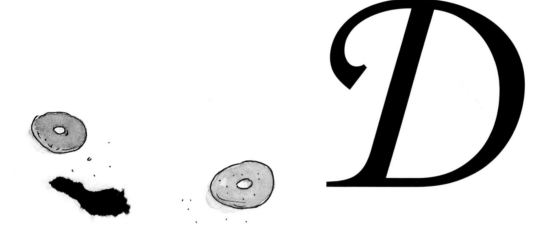

D

David the dog-faced boy, dingy and dirty,
Tried to look dapper by donning a derby.

Excellent Edward, exceedingly picky,

Ate eggs with an eel whose earwax was icky.

F

Friday when Frank fixed frijoles and French fries
His fiancée Franny was covered in fruit flies.

G

While Granny in Greenland had gravlax for three,

Her gallant son Gary grew green gracefully.

H

Henrietta the hare wore a habit in heaven,
Her hairdo hid hunchbacks: one hundred and seven.

I

Iggy's aunt Ida, indecent in undies,
Hid icicles under her Indian uncle.

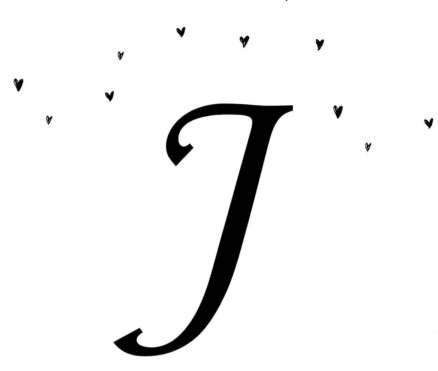

J

Josie from Jupiter jailed Jerry Johnson
For joking with Jack and his jerky son Jason.

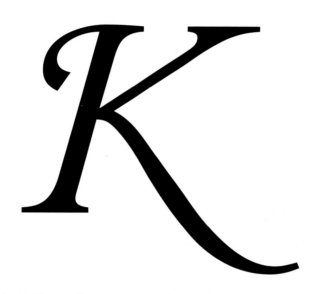

Kathy and Keith kayaked to Kansas

Though they were told not to by King Kong's aunt Frances.

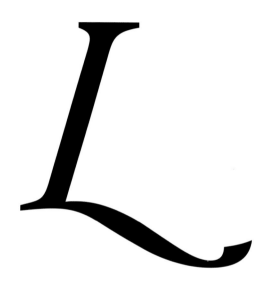

L

Lovely Lorraine lost loud Larry's locket
Then found it again in long Louie's pocket.

M

Maniacal Marvin munched many a macaroon,

Making his middle a mini hot air balloon.

N

Needle-nosed Nigel won nine kinds of knockwurst

By winning a contest to see who could knock worst.

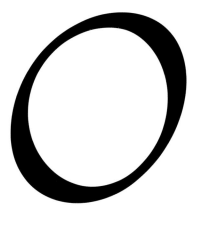

Old Ollie the owl owed Owen an oboe

But instead bought him oysters at Osgood's in Soho.

P

Pedro the puppy piled poop on his paws

And Papa dog published his photo because.

Quincy the kumquat queried the queen
Cleverly, quietly, without being seen.

R

Roberta the robot, resplendent in rubies,
Rehearsed her recital and sang "Rootie Tootie!"

Sour notes so badly sung by sopranos

Sank a seaworthy sloop that was shipping pianos.

T

Tough Tommy told Tina, who tiptoed in toe shoes,
"Take time for tea and I'll try on your tutu."

$\mathcal{U}$

Odd Uncle U-Ball, never the sanest,
Uplifted himself to the planet Uranus.

In varsity Victor was often victorious—
Sadly, his winning made him vainglorious.

W

Double-U's wonderful but it worries me
Shouldn't it weally be called Double-V?

X

Ambidextrous Alex was actually axed

For waxing, then faxing, his boss's new slacks.

Y

...IT'S YUMMY!

YELENA'S YOGURT

YAM

Yesterday Yuri the yeti did yoga,

Today he spilled yogurt all over his toga.

Zany Zeno zoomed to the end zone,

But with a zucchini, scoring him zero.

FLYING DOLPHIN PRESS

PUBLISHED BY DOUBLEDAY/FLYING DOLPHIN PRESS

E
MAR

Published in the United States by Doubleday/Flying Dolphin Press, an imprint of The Doubleday Broadway
Publishing Group, a division of Random House, Inc., New York.
www.doubleday.com

DOUBLEDAY/FLYING DOLPHIN PRESS and its colophon are trademarks of Random House, Inc.

Library of Congress Cataloging-in-Publication Data

Martin, Steve, 1945–
The alphabet from A to Y with bonus letter Z! /by Steve Martin &Roz Chast.—1st ed.
p. cm.
Summary: Presents a rhyming couplet featuring each letter of the alphabet, with such characters as David
the dog-faced boy, who dons a derby despite being dirty, and Victor, whose frequent victories have made
him vainglorious.
[1. Behavior—Fiction. 2. Alphabet. 3. Humorous stories. 4. Stories in rhyme.] I. Chast, Roz, ill. II. Title.

PZ8.3.M418585Alp 2007
[E]—dc22
2006102543

ISBN 978-0-385-51662-4 (trade)
ISBN 987-0-385-52377-6 (lib. bdg.)

PRINTED IN THE UNITED STATES OF AMERICA

1 3 5 7 9 10 8 6 4 2

First Edition

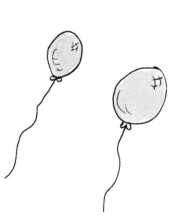

ORLAND PARK
PUBLIC LIBRARY
A Natural Connection

14921 Ravinia Avenue
Orland Park, IL 60462

708-428-5100
orlandparklibrary.org